This Annual belongs to

Princess.............................

(Write your name here)

Editor: Sally Gilbert
Art Editor: Alexandra Chamadia
Photography: Laura Ashman

© Disney Enterprises, Inc. All rights reserved. Published in Great Britain in 2005 by Egmont Books Limited, 239 Kensington High Street, London W8 6SA. Printed in Italy.
1 3 5 7 9 10 8 6 4 2
ISBN 1 4052 2101 1
Note to parents: adult supervision is recommended when sharp-pointed items such as scissors are in use.

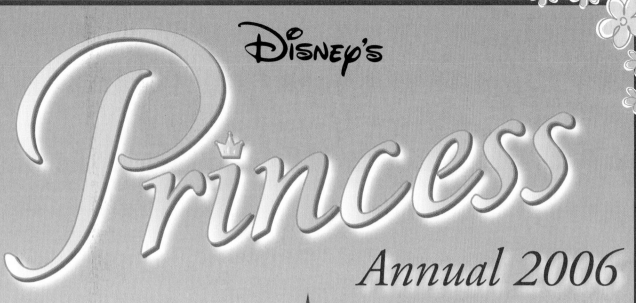

Disney's

Princess

Annual 2006

*O*nce upon a time, in fairy tale kingdoms far away, there lived seven beautiful princesses.

8   *Meet Snow White*
9   *Read Snow White's story*
12   *Make Snow White's tiara*
13   *Solve Snow White's puzzle*
14   *Complete Snow White's colouring*
15   *Forest Fun*

16   *Meet Aurora*
17   *Enjoy Aurora's story*
20   *Create Aurora's brooch*
21   *Colour Aurora's picture*
22   *Solve Aurora's puzzles*
23   *Fairy Teasers*

24   *Meet Cinderella*
25   *Read Cinderella's story*
28   *Make Cinderella's invites*
29   *Try Cinderella's puzzles*
30   *Finish Cinderella's colouring*
31   *Friendship Quiz*

32 *Meet Ariel*
33 *Enjoy Ariel's story*
36 *Create Ariel's chest*
37 *Draw Ariel's treasure*
38 *Play Ariel's game*
39 *Fishy Facts*

40 *Meet Jasmine*
41 *Read Jasmine's story*
44 *Make Jasmine's ring*
45 *Find the route through the maze*
46 *Finish Jasmine's colouring*
47 *Animal Antics*

48 *Meet Belle*
49 *Enjoy Belle's story*
52 *Create Belle's pendant*
53 *Complete Belle's colouring*
54 *Solve Belle's puzzle*
55 *Enchanted Puzzles*

56 *Meet Mulan*
57 *Read Mulan's story*
60 *Make Mulan's fan*
61 *Try Mulan's puzzles*
62 *Finish Mulan's colouring*
63 *Chinese Capers*

64 *Play our kites and dragons game*
66 *Read your princess horoscopes*
68 *Try our princess quiz*

Turn the page to begin the fairy tale...

Snow White Factfile

Personality: Friendly and
kind-hearted

Appearance: Milky-white skin
and rosy cheeks

Romance: Prince Charming

Family: The wicked Queen

Friends: The seven dwarfs:
Grumpy, Happy,
Sneezy, Doc, Bashful,
Sleepy and Dopey.
The forest creatures

Favourite phrase: "Want to
know a secret?"

Crown of Confidence

Enjoy reading this story about the royal parade.

One day, Snow White and the Prince were invited to lead a parade through the whole kingdom. "Everyone will be there, so we will have to be at our most impressive," the Prince chuckled.

At first, Snow White felt excited about the parade. Once she was alone, however, she began thinking about being the focus of such a big event.

"The entire kingdom will be looking at me," she thought to herself.

"What if I fall over?"

Later, she tried on all her prettiest gowns but Snow White still felt that there was something missing. She decided to take her mind off the parade by going to visit her friends, the dwarfs.

When she arrived at the mine, Snow White was surprised to find that each of the dwarfs was working in a different area. "Why don't you all dig in the same place?" she puzzled.

"Because we're all digging for different jewels," laughed Happy. "My favourite is the diamond."

"Blue sapphires are best," giggled Doc.

"Green emeralds are better than anything," added Sneezy.

Dopey, Sleepy, Bashful and Grumpy showed Snow White their rubies, opals, onyx and amethysts.

Snow White couldn't help laughing, as the dwarfs kept squabbling over which jewel was the best. "They're all lovely, just like you," she laughed. Snow White was happy that the dwarfs had made her forget about her worries for a while. "If only you were all with me at the front of the royal parade," she said.

"But the parade is for you and the Prince. It wouldn't look right with us marching with you," said Happy.

"I suppose, but I'd feel extra confident knowing my friends were right with me," Snow White sighed.

"You should go home now, Snow White," declared Grumpy, "we've got to go back to work in the mine."

The other dwarfs thought Grumpy was being rude to Snow White but he wasn't. As soon as she had left, Grumpy told the others his plan.

The day of the parade arrived and Snow White nervously got ready in her room.

Even though she looked stunning, she still felt worried about the parade.

As she came out of the palace, the dwarfs were waiting by the gates.

"Are you going to join me in the parade?" she asked, excitedly.

The dwarfs shook their heads but produced a crown that was encrusted with all their favourite jewels.

"It's wonderful," cried Snow White. "Now, I'll know my friends are right with me when I'm wearing the crown."

The dwarfs were delighted, as Snow White confidently set off for the parade with her prince.

The End

11

Jewelled Tiara

Make Snow White's glittering jewelled tiara.

 1 Draw and cut out a tiara shape from pink card.

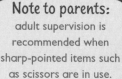

2 Decorate the tiara by gluing on coloured jewels.

3 Tape the tiara into shape, ensuring that it fits around your head.

Charming Changes

These two pictures may look the same but there are six changes to the lower one. Can you spot them all?

13

14 Use the little picture in the flower to help you colour this scene.

Forest Fun

Circle the answers to this Snow White quiz, then complete the fill-ins below.

 1 How many dwarfs are there?

   A Four
   B Eight
   C Seven

 2 Which dwarf doesn't speak?

   A Dopey
   B Doc
   C Happy

My Princess Factfile

My name: ....

....

My age: ....

My address: ....

....

....

Answers:
1-C, 2-A.

15

Aurora Factfile

Personality: Aurora is a bit of a dreamer

Appearance: She has a sparkling smile

Romance: Prince Phillip

Family: King Stefan and the Queen

Friends: The Fairy Godmothers: Flora, Fauna and Merryweather. The forest creatures

Favourite phrase: "If you dream a dream more than once, it is bound to come true."

Anniversary Gown

Read this story about Aurora's special gown.

It was a few days before the anniversary of Aurora's marriage to Prince Phillip. To celebrate, the Prince had organised a romantic ball at the palace.

"Everyone we know will be there," said Prince Phillip. "I want them all to see how happy we are."

Aurora decided that the gown she wore should reflect their happiness. "I want it to capture the spirit of the day when we first met," she told the fairies.

The fairies became very excited about the anniversary gown and rushed to give Aurora their suggestions.

"Your gown should definitely be green," declared Fauna, "like the fresh, spring grass you and the Prince stood upon on that first meeting."

"No, it should be pink like the roses the Prince picked for you," protested Flora.

"Fiddlesticks, it's obvious that the gown should be blue, like the bright blue sky on

the day you met!" insisted Merryweather.

Before long, the three fairies were squabbling so much that Aurora couldn't hear herself think.

"I'll go into the forest," thought Aurora, "I'm sure to get some inspiration there."

As Aurora walked, the forest creatures came out to greet her.

"You were all there the day I met the Prince," she said. "What colour do you think best captures the day?"

Just like the fairies, each of the forest creatures had a different opinion about what colour the anniversary gown should be. The array of wonderfully coloured butterflies, birds and flowers made Aurora's choice even harder.

"There are so many colours they are making me feel dizzy," she fretted. It was all becoming too much for Aurora, so she decided to go and sit quietly until she calmed down and could think straight. She sat alone on a rock that looked out over the forest.

The scenery was very beautiful and she instantly felt much better.

"All this fuss just for a gown," she giggled. Then she thought about her very favourite moment of the day she met the Prince.

"He gave me a kiss and I felt so happy, I lit up like a rainbow," she sighed.

Aurora suddenly gasped with delight, as she realised that she had found the perfect design for her gown.

"One colour isn't enough to show how happy we are, we need lots of them," she cried, happily.

On the day of her anniversary ball, Aurora's rainbow gown looked spectacular. The fairies and the forest creatures all agreed that it was an absolutely perfect choice.

When the proud prince kissed Aurora in front of the guests, everyone could see how bright their love shone.

The End

Butterfly Brooch

Make this pretty brooch - it will make your heart flutter.

You will need:

pink card

sticky tape

scissors

sequins

glue

brooch clasp

pencil

1 Draw a butterfly shape on to pink card and carefully it cut out.

2 Decorate the butterfly shape by sticking on lots of sequins.

3 Glue a brooch clasp to the back of your butterfly brooch and ask an adult to pin it to your outfit.

Use the little picture in Merryweather's magic spell to
help you colour this picture.

Magic Mayhem

Aurora is trying to count how many
spells the fairies have cast.

Find the number that appears three times
below to find out.

3　　6

3　　　8　　　12

10　16　　　　12　　15

12

8　15　　　　　4　　7

16　　　　　　7

Answer:
The fairies have cast 12 spells.

Fairy Teasers

Can you answer these questions about Aurora's fairy friends, then complete the fill-ins below.

 1 What colour outfit does Fauna wear?

A Green
B Blue
C Pink

 2 The fairies live in a.......?

A Castle
B Cottage
C Bungalow

My Princess Looks

Height: ....

Hair: ....

Eyes: ....

Shoe size: ....

Distinctive Marks: ....

....

Cinderella Factfile

Personality: Cinderella is nice and kind

Appearance: Stunningly elegant blue-eyed blonde

Romance: Prince Charming

Friends: Gus and Jaq, the mice. The forest birds

Family: Father; stepsisters, Anastasia and Drizella; and stepmother, Lady Tremaine

Favourite phrase: "If you tell a wish it won't come true."

The Winter Party

Read all about Cinderella's special event.

At the start of each winter, Cinderella and the Prince held a spectacular winter party to celebrate the changing of the seasons.

The winter party was famous throughout the kingdom and it was all anyone talked about for weeks beforehand.

This made Anastasia and Drizella very jealous. "We'll have our own party on the same day this year, and then everyone in the kingdom will be talking about us instead," hissed Drizella.

"Great idea, I'm sure it will be really easy to organise a party!" sniggered Anastasia.

The sisters made up invitations that promised the guests a magical event. "We'll send them out early to all the people who normally go to Cinderella's winter party," cackled Drizella.

"We can send the last invitation to Cinderella just before her party is due to start!" chuckled Anastasia.

But organising a big party was much harder than Anastasia and Drizella

expected. The decorations they put up kept falling down, the punch they made tasted worse than puddle water and when they looked at the long list of guests, they realised their ballroom was going to be far too small.

By the day of the party, Anastasia and Drizella were panicking.

"This is going to be an absolute disaster," gulped Anastasia.

"Everyone in the kingdom will be talking about us for all the wrong reasons," wailed Drizella.

Meanwhile, Cinderella had just finished preparing her own party when she opened her invitation to Anastasia's and Drizella's party. She realised that no one would be coming to her party but Cinderella didn't get upset.

"I always feel special when people come to my parties," she thought. "Anastasia and Drizella will get a turn at feeling special when people go to theirs."

Cinderella decided to go and help her

stepsisters with any final preparations.

But when she arrived, nothing was ready. Anastasia and Drizella were sobbing behind the curtains.

"It's all gone wrong. People will laugh at our terrible party," spluttered Drizella.

Cinderella couldn't help but feel sorry for her two stepsisters. "I'd be really honoured if you held your party at my palace," said Cinderella, "everything is already prepared."

The sisters were so grateful for

Cinderella's kindness that they forgot all about being jealous and began to enjoy themselves, as they redirected the guests to Cinderella's palace.

Before long, the party was under way and all the guests were having a great time. The guests congratulated Anastasia and Drizella for organising a fantastic night.

"We could never have done it without the kindness of Cinderella," they said.

The End

27

Party Invites

Make these princess hat invites to
send to your friends.

You will need:

scissors

coloured card
or paper

beads &
sequins

gold ribbon

glue

pencil

glitter glue

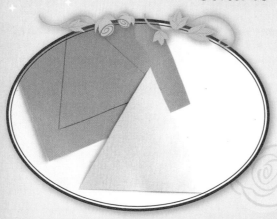

1 Draw a triangular
princess hat shape on
to coloured card and
carefully cut it out.

Note to parents:
adult supervision is
recommended when
sharp-pointed items
such as scissors
are in use.

2 Cut out a smaller paper
triangle and stick
it on to your triangle.

3 Decorate your princess
hat with sequins, gold
ribbon and glitter glue.

Princess
....
Invites you
to a party on
....
At.................
....
Wear a tiara. RSVP

Princess
....
Invites you
to a party on
....
At.................
....
Wear a tiara. RSVP

28

Royal Ball

Cinderella is dancing the night away with her prince.

Can you spot which shadow matches them exactly?

Use the little picture in the heart to help you colour this scene.

Friendship Quiz

Circle the answers to this quiz, then complete
the fill-ins below.

 1 Who are Cinderella's
mice friends?

A Gus and Jaq
B Jack and Jill
C Gav and Jack

 2 Who are Anastasia
and Drizella?

A Cinderella's cousins
B Cinderella's friends
C Cinderella's stepsisters

Princess Friends

My best friend is: ....

....

I like her because: ....

....

....

Ariel Factfile

Personality: Ariel is impulsive and independent

Appearance: Bright red hair and blue eyes

Romance: Prince Eric

Friends: Flounder, the guppy fish; Sebastian, the crab; Scuttle, the seagull

Family: King Triton, her father; her six sisters: Adella, Andrina, Alana, Aquata, Attina, Arista

Favourite phrase: "It's so much more fun above the waves."

The Shipwreck

Read Ariel's exiting adventure under the sea.

One night, during a terrible storm at sea, a grand ship was blown on to the jagged rocks. Ariel watched the people on board clamber into lifeboats and row to the shore. Ariel noticed a pretty girl who looked heartbroken, as the ship slipped below the surface of the waves.

"She must have left something very special behind," thought Ariel.

The next morning, when the sea was calm, Ariel and Flounder went to explore the sunken ship.

"Wow, that girl must have been a princess," said Flounder, as they swam around the ship's elaborate corridors. Suddenly, they heard tapping coming from one of the cabins.

"What's that?" gulped Flounder.

"There's only one way to find out," whispered Ariel, as she opened the door.

To their astonishment, there was a large fish tank containing two spectacular pink fish with frilly fins and blue eyes. The fish couldn't get out, because there was a latch on the lid of the tank. Ariel rushed over and set them free.

"Thank goodness you found us," said one of the fish.

"We've got to get back to Princess Madeline,

she'll be missing us," added the other fish.

"You're at the bottom of the ocean, she'll think you're lost for ever," said Flounder.

"True friends never give up on each other," said Ariel and led the two fish up to the surface. They instantly spotted a palace on a hill.

"That's where Princess Madeline lives," cried the first fish.

"But we'll never be able to reach it," sighed the second fish.

"Like I said, friends don't give up on each other," giggled Ariel. She pointed at Princess Madeline who was standing on the shore, sadly looking out to sea.

The two fish swam towards her.

Princess Madeline wept with happiness when she saw the pink fish coming towards her. "I thought I'd never see you again but I wished and wished and my wish came true!" exclaimed Princess Madeline. She told the two fish to wait, while she went and fetched a bowl to carry them back to the palace.

As soon as she was gone, the fish darted back to Ariel and Flounder. "We could

never have found Madeline without your help," said the first fish.

"If Princess Madeline knew how kind you've been, she'd want to reward you. So we'll tell you about her secret room on the ship so you can collect your thank-you gift from her," giggled the second fish.

A short while later, Madeline returned and the fish said goodbye to Ariel and Flounder. Ariel felt happy as she watched Princess Madeline scoop them up and carry them away.

"I wonder what's in the secret room?" asked Flounder.

"Let's go and see," chuckled Ariel. They followed the fish's directions around the ship until they came to a large bookcase. When Ariel pressed in a pink book, the bookcase opened like a door and revealed a room full of dazzling jewellery and beautiful dresses.

"These wonderful princess gifts will help us to remember this adventure forever and ever," cried Ariel.

The End

Treasure Chest

Create this pretty chest for all your princess treasures.

You will need:

scissors

wrapping paper

box

beads

cord

glue

 1 Neatly cover the box with wrapping paper.

2 Make the box look like a chest by gluing on lengths of cord.

3 Finally, decorate the chest by sticking on lots of jewels.

In the space above, draw what you think Ariel
has found in the treasure chest.

Memory Game

Test your memory with Ariel.

How good is your memory? To test yourself, study this page for three minutes, then cover it up with a piece of paper. Write down as many objects as you can remember. No cheating!

Fishy Facts

Solve these tricky teasers and then complete the fill-ins below.

 1 What colour is Ariel's friend, Flounder?

A Yellow and pink
B Yellow and blue
C Yellow and green

 2 Which creature is Sebastian?

A A lobster
B A guppy fish
C A crab

My favourite things

My favourite book: ....

....

My best-loved toy: ....

....

My favourite colour: ....

....

Jasmine Factfile

Personality: Jasmine is smart, fun and beautiful

Appearance: Long dark hair and exotic eyes

Romance: Aladdin

Family: Her father, the Sultan

Friends: Rajah the tiger, Abu the monkey

Lives: The Sultan's palace in Agrabah

Favourite phrase: "If I do marry, then I want it to be for love."

Princess Creations

Aladdin helps Jasmine show everyone
her artistic side.

One day, Aladdin went to visit Jasmine on his magic carpet.

Jasmine didn't see him landing on the balcony, because she was completely engrossed in her embroidery.

Aladdin watched Jasmine, as she confidently stitched away. He was really impressed by how artistic Jasmine was. Embroidery was just one skill in a long list of artistic talents. "You're very creative," he whispered.

Jasmine was thrilled to see him and was very flattered by his comments.

"I think more people should see your work," added Aladdin.

"Sometimes, the officials who visit the palace see my work," replied Jasmine.

"I'm not just talking about a few rich people who are lucky enough to come to the palace, I mean everyone in the city of Agrabah!" declared Aladdin.

Jasmine liked the idea of her artistic talents being seen by lots of people but she felt it would be impossible, because she wasn't allowed out of the palace.

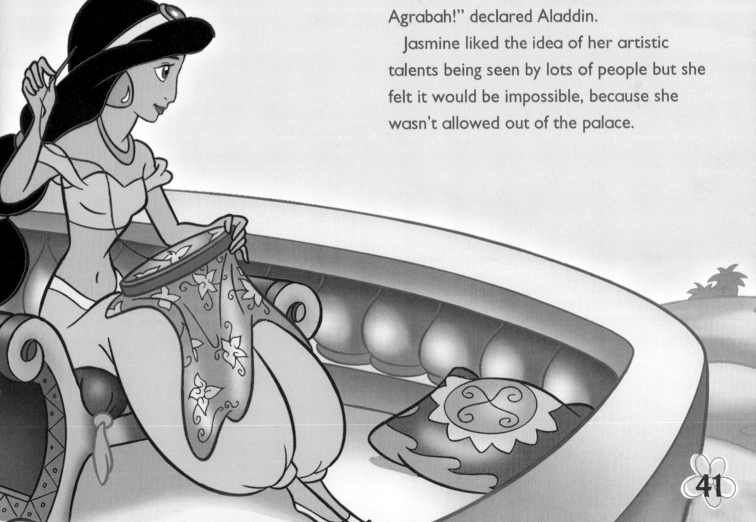

"Even if I was able to take my work outside, where would I show it? There are no exhibitions and most people are too busy to come and see it," sighed Jasmine.

"There must be a way to get your work to a wider audience," insisted Aladdin. Then he looked down at his magic carpet and had an idea.

"How would you like your work to be seen by every single person in the city?" he said, smiling.

Jasmine grinned with curiosity, as Aladdin took her by the hand and led her on to the magic carpet.

"You steer," said Aladdin, as they took off and headed towards a huge shapeless cloud floating over the city. Jasmine smiled as she understood what Aladdin wanted her to do. She used the whizzing carpet to shave and carve the edges off the cloud. Soon she had created a wonderful image of the royal palace. The people in the city below stopped what they were doing and looked up in

amazement at the beautiful work of art.

When Jasmine landed back on her balcony, she curtsied to the crowd. She was thrilled when they began to clap and whistle their appreciation.

"Thanks, Aladdin for getting my art seen by everyone in Agrabah," said Jasmine.

"I think your art is going to be seen in cities all over the world," replied Aladdin, as the palace-shaped cloud floated off into the distance.

The End

Jasmine's Ring

Make this stunning ring and sparkle with eastern magic.

You will need:

silver card

pencil

scissors

glue

blue beads

jewel

1 Draw and cut a small circle from silver card to make the top of your ring.

2 Stick blue beads and a jewel to the card circle.

3 Make the band of the ring from a strip of silver card. Stick the band to the back of the ring.

Note to parents: adult supervision is recommended when sharp-pointed items such as scissors are in use.

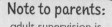

Magic Carpet Maze

Jasmine and Aladdin need to get home after their adventures. Which route should they take?

Answer:
Route c.

Use the little picture in the tree to help you colour this scene.

Animal Antics

Answer these Jasmine questions, then fill in the questions below.

 **1** What animal is Rajah?

A A monkey
B A tiger
C A lion

 2 Whose pet monkey is Abu?

A Jasmine's
B Aladdin's
C The Sultan's

Animal Friends

My favourite animals or pets: ....

....

I love them because: ....

....

My favourite animal name is: ....

....

Answers:
1-B, 2-B.

47

Belle factfile

Personality: Belle is intelligent, loyal and brave

Appearance: Beautiful brown eyes and hair

Romance: The Beast

Family: Her father, Maurice

Friends: Lumiere, Chip, Cogsworth, Mrs Potts, Mrs Wardrobe and Feather Duster

Favourite phrase: "I just finished a wonderful story."

The Perfect Gift

Belle has trouble finding a present for the Beast.

One day, Belle decided that she wanted to give the Beast a special gift for all the kindness he had shown her.

"Maybe the Beast would like a new jacket?" she thought. But then Belle looked in his wardrobe and saw that he already had enough jackets to wear a different one on each day of the month! "I'll have to think of something else," she puzzled.

"He might like some sweet-smelling bath salts," thought Belle. But then she found out that the Beast already had every possible kind of bath salt in his bathroom.

Each time Belle thought of a something she could give to the Beast, she quickly discovered that he already had it. Belle was soon at her wit's end and realised there was only one thing to do. She would ask the Beast himself.

"You have so many things. I really don't

know what gift to give you," she confessed.

"Your friendship is the best gift I could ever have," replied the Beast.

Belle was very flattered but she still wanted to give him something. Then she had a thought. "I know, I can give you a kiss on the cheek to show my friendship," she cheered. Belle leaned forward to kiss the Beast's cheek but he stopped her.

"Wait! If you are going to give me a kiss, I want you to do it in the West Wing of the castle," he said, softly.

"Why?" puzzled Belle.

"Because there will be a gift there for you," he replied.

When they reached the West Wing, Belle was surprised when the Beast lifted the delicate glass cover off the enchanted rose. He leaned over the rose and whispered, "I'll have my gift now."

Belle smiled as she leaned forward and kissed him on the cheek.

The Beast sighed and a single tear of happiness rolled down his face and fell on to the enchanted rose.

Belle gasped when the rose glowed and the teardrop hardened into a dazzling tear-shaped diamond! The Beast picked it up and attached the diamond tear to a beautiful silver chain.

Belle was thrilled as he placed the chain around her neck. "This diamond will always sparkle as brightly as our friendship," said the Beast.

"And just like our friendship, I'll keep it close to my heart," replied Belle.

The End

Pretty Pendant

Make and wear this pretty pendant and you can glitter like a princess, too.

1 Cut out a pendant shape from silver card, cutting out a hole in the top.

Note to parents: adult supervision is recommended when sharp-pointed items such as scissors are in use.

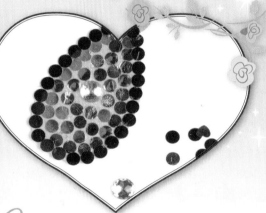

2 Glue lots of sequins and jewels on to the pendant.

3 Thread a length of silver ribbon through the hole in the top of your princess pendant to hang it around your neck.

Use the picture in the castle to help you colour this scene.

53

Love is in the Air

Belle and the Beast are enjoying a romantic day together.

How many times can you find the word LOVE in the
jumbled letters below? Each letter can only be used once.

E
D
L T I E S K S B A
L O T D L H S P E
L O V L L B H J O B
T K E G O B F G H L O V E
S A E J L K L B S
M V M
E

Answer:
The word 'LOVE' appears three times.

Enchanted Puzzles

Answer these questions, then complete the fun fill-ins.

1 Who is Mrs Potts' son?

A Chop
B Chip
C Chap

2 What was the Beast before the spell was cast on him?

A A sailor
B A prince
C A king

All about you

Where do you live? : ....

....

....

Is there anywhere else you'd

like to live? : ....

....

....

Mulan Factfile

Personality: Mulan is a bit of tomboy at heart

Appearance: Stylish and elegant

Romance: Shang

Family: Her father, Fa Zhou, mother, Fa Li and Grandma Fa

Friends: Khan the horse, Mushu the dragon, Cri-Kee the cricket and Little Brother the dog

Favourite phrase: "I have to keep up my family honour."

The Emperor's Visit

Read this story about the Emperor visiting Mulan's village.

One day, an exciting proclamation announced that the Emperor was coming to Mulan's province. He wanted to meet his subjects and see for himself how they lived. The proclamation went on to explain that to avoid an overwhelming crowd, only one member of each family was invited to the lavish ceremony in the village where they would meet the Emperor.

Mulan knew her father greatly admired the Emperor and would think it a great honour to meet him. So she was surprised when her father told her that she would be the one to go from their family.

"But you might not get another chance to meet him," said Mulan.

"I couldn't go anyway, I have to stay and work the fields," said her father.

Mulan was very excited and began thinking about which dress she would wear to the event. Just then, she saw her father in his room, proudly looking at his old army uniform. Mulan realised that her father was sacrificing his own wish just for her.

"Father, I know you are letting me go in your place, because you love me. Now let me show you the same love and insist you go instead," she said.

"But what about the harvest in the field?" said her father.

"I would be honoured to do the work for you," Mulan smiled.

Her father smiled with pride at Mulan's selfless heart.

The next day, her father left for the ceremony, wearing his polished uniform.

Mulan went out into the fields and began working. She started thinking about the ceremony and wondered what it would have been like. Mulan pretended an old scarecrow was the Emperor and performed a graceful dance before it. When she finished, she gave the scarecrow an elegant curtsy.

"Very entertaining," chuckled a dry voice from the road next to the field.

Mulan turned and saw an old man in a shabby hooded cloak shuffling along towards the village.

"Are you on your way to the Emperor's ceremony?" asked Mulan.

"Yes," he replied.

It was a hot day and the old man looked frail, so Mulan told him to rest for a moment and offered him some cool water.

The old man accepted and asked why such a pretty girl was working the fields. Mulan laughed and explained what she had done for her father.

"That was a very noble thing to do. I am

very glad that I chose to walk this way and met you," said the old man.

Mulan gasped with astonishment, as he lifted his hood and revealed that he was, in fact, the Emperor.

"Why are you out here walking alone?" spluttered Mulan.

"When I arrive at a big ceremony, everyone automatically treats me like an Emperor. But you showed me respect and honesty without knowing who I was," he explained. The Emperor asked Mulan to accompany him to the ceremony.

Mulan asked the Emperor if they could stop off at her house first, so she could get changed into the dress she had already chosen for the ceremony. The Emperor laughed but agreed.

Later, Mulan's father swelled with pride when she introduced him to the Emperor.

"If the people of this province are anything like your daughter Mulan," said the Emperor, "then this must be the most honourable place in all of China."

The End

59

Fabulous Fan

Make this pretty fan from old wrapping paper.

You will need:

wrapping paper

sticky tape

scissors

stapler

ribbon

1 Fold a rectangle of wrapping paper like a concertina.

2 Staple or tape the bottom ends together and tie a ribbon around them.

Note to parents: adult supervision is recommended when sharp-pointed items such as scissors are in use.

Lovely Lanterns

Mulan loves to decorate her home with beautiful lanterns.

Help her count how many lanterns there are below.

Answer:
There are 16 lanterns, including the one Mulan is holding.

Use the picture in the little parasol to help you colour this pretty scene.

Chinese Capers

Answer these tricky questions, then complete the fill-ins below.

1 What is Mulan's horse called?

A Can
B Khan
C Dapple

2 Who is Mulan's relation, Fa Zhou?

A Mulan's father
B Mulan's mother
C Mulan's grandma

My favourite princess

My favourite princess is: ....

....

....

To be like her I must: ....

....

....

Kites and Dragons

Who's going to be the first to win? Play this game

How to play

You will need: a counter for each player and a dice. Each player places their counter on the Start. Next, players take it in turn to roll the dice and move their counter forward the correct number of places. Remember, if you land on a dragon's head, you go down its tail.
If you land on a kite's tail, you climb it. The first player to reach the finish square is the winner.

Princess Horoscopes

Tiaras
23rd Dec - 20th Jan

Tiaras are always bubbling with creative energy. Make some crafts for your friends.

Roses
21st Jan - 19th Feb

Roses have a gift when it comes to gardening. Plant some seeds and see how they grow.

Slippers
20th Feb - 20th Mar

There is a special treat in store for Slippers. This may come in the form of a surprise.

Lamps
21st Mar - 20th Apr

Lamps will be asked some tricky questions. They'll come through with flying colours.

Shells
21st Apr - 21st May

Shells are going to have lots of fantastic luck. Don't forget to share your good fortune.

Jewels
22nd May - 21st June

Jewels always love to see others smile. They make someone's dreams come true.

Diamonds
22nd June - 23rd July

Diamonds will stumble on a mystery. They may solve it, or it could lead to an adventure.

Stars
24th July - 23rd Aug

Stars will take part in a big party. They will have lots of fun and dance till their feet are tired.

Wands
24th Aug - 23rd Sep

A close friend will ask for advice. It's good that Wands are the perfect listeners.

Carriages
24th Sep - 23rd Oct

Carriages are brilliant at baking. They are going to cook up a treat for someone special.

Waterlilies
24th Oct - 22nd Nov

Waterlilies will have a special friend to visit. Together they will have a great girly giggle.

Wild flowers
23rd Nov - 22nd Dec

Wild flowers will go on a journey. They love adventure, so they will have a fantastic time.

Princess Quiz

Which princess are you most like? Try our quiz and find out.

START

Have you more boyfriends than girlfriends?

Yes → Do you like rare animals?

No → Do you like wearing your hair down?

Do you like rare animals?
No → Do you like cooking?
Yes → Do you like dressmaking?

Do you like cooking?
Yes → Do you like exotic food?
No → Do you like woodland walks?

Do you like exotic food?
No
Yes

Do you like dressmaking?
No → Do you like woodland walks?
Yes → Do you like ballgowns?

Do you like wearing your hair down?
No

Do you like ballgowns?
Yes
No

Do you like woodland walks?
Yes

Do you enjoy adventures?
Yes
No

68

Are you always happy?

Yes

Do you like forest creatures?

Yes

No

No

Yes

Snow White

You are just like happy Snow White. You love the simple things in life.

Yes

Are you a good organiser?

No

Do you like visiting new places?

No

Jasmine

Just like Jasmine, you like to visit new places and have lots of fun.

Yes

No

No

Do you like mice?

Do you like housework?

Yes

Yes

Cinderella

You work hard like Cinderella. You also like lovely things, too.

69